the knights of Boo'Gar

Story & Art By
Art Roche

Andrews McMeel
Publishing®
a division of Andrews McMeel Universal

Andrews McMeel Publishing
a division of Andrews McMeel Universal
1130 Walnut Street, Kansas City, Missouri 64106

www.andrewsmcmeel.com

17 18 19 20 21 SDB 10 9 8 7 6 5 4 3 2 1

ISBN: 978-1-4494-7987-9

Library of Congress Control Number: 2016946799

Made by:
Shenzhen Donnelley Printing Company Ltd.
Address and location of manufacturer:
No. 47, Wuhe Nan Road, Bantian Ind. Zone,
Shenzhen China, 518129
1st Printing – 1/9/17

Editor: Dorothy O'Brien
Designer: Brenna Thummler
Creative Director: Tim Lynch
Production Manager: Chuck Harper
Production Editor: Maureen Sullivan

Acknowledgments

This book is dedicated to my wife, Elizabeth, and my sons, Arthur and John. May I always endeavor to make your kingdom a proud and happy one.

I would also offer thanks to the friends who gave me so much encouragement and support: Paige Braddock, Lex Fajardo, Alena Carnes, Vicki Scott, and Brian Fies, thank you for your ideas and endless enthusiasm. Thanks also to Andrea Colvin, an editor bold enough to take a chance on a book about medieval boogers.

I'm grateful to my story editor, Michael Wexler, who endured my snippy e-mails and steadfastly guided me through my own creative bog and onto dry land. And to the fantastic team at Andrews McMeel, particularly Dorothy O'Brien, Shelly Barkes, Tim Lynch, and Kirsty Melville.

You guys are the greatest.

Chapter 1

The morning sun shone through the tall windows of Castle Boo'Gar as King Mewkus and his faithful wizard, Edwart, sat in the game room playing a relaxing game of Castles and Cantaloupes.

"You can't move your game piece like that," said King Mewkus.

"Yes, I can," said Edwart. "I rolled a nine, which gives me the Charm of Dexterity."

"The Charm of Dexterity is on a seven roll," replied the king.

"Yes, but I captured a Pixie of Ripeness on my last move. That makes all my rolls a seven," snapped the wizard.

The king was outraged. "Where did you find a Pixie of Ripeness in the Cave of the Anxious Beaver? That's not even possible!"

"Your Majesty," replied his old friend calmly, "I do wish you'd learn the rules of this game. We've been playing every morning for nine years."

The king tossed his game piece to one side and slumped back in his chair. "Well . . . I wish you didn't have those bushy eyebrows. Too bad wishes don't come true."

Suddenly the door to the game room burst open.

"FATHER!" shouted Princess Phlema. "FATHER! He's GONE!"

The startled king knocked over his cup of turnip tea, spilling it on the carpet. "Oh dear, Phlema," said the annoyed king. "Now look what you've done."

"FATHER!" screamed Phlema. "Babycakes is not in his pen. He's been taken!"

The king dabbed at the carpet with a faded lace napkin. "Calm down, my sparkling jewel. I'm sure you're mistaken."

"Who is Babycakes, may I ask?" inquired the wizard.

Princess Phlema turned to Edwart, her royal lip quivering with heartfelt emotion. "Baby-cakes is the sweetest, smartest goat in the royal stable. I've grown quite fond of him, so this is a major disaster! I may cry myself to DEATH!" wailed the distraught teenager.

With that, the highly excitable Princess Phlema fell to the ground and melted into a puddle of sobbing and crying.

"WHAAAAAAAAAAAaaaaaaaaaaaa!"

The wizard looked over at the king. "A goat?" said Edwart.

"MY BABY!" wailed Princess Phlema.

The king stood up, looking at Edwart. He rolled his eyes ever so slightly. "There, there now, my daughter," said the king. "I'm sure he just wandered off to find some tasty grass to nibble on. Rest easy, my dear."

King Mewkus looked down and weakly patted his daughter on the shoulder.

"No! He's been taken!" sobbed the princess. "This morning I went to check on him—to give him his oatmeal and tell him a story," she cried. "This is a disaster! What cruel villain . . . what insane nut job would steal an innocent goat? WHAAAAAAAAAaaaaaaa!"

"Perhaps someone who likes cheese?" the wizard offered helpfully.

The king stood up and thought for a moment, touching the golden key that sparkled on a chain around his neck. "Who indeed? There are many cheese lovers in Boo'Gar . . . but to steal a royal goat? That is bold. An act of defiance, really," the king said, his voice rising.

The king's cheeks flushed with anger. Edwart looked at him with alarm. "Calm down, Your Highness," said Edwart.

"This will not stand!" said King Mewkus, pounding the game table with his fist. "I am the king, and people should keep their mitts off my property. This is an outrage!"

"We're still talking about a goat, right?" asked the wizard.

"DO SOMETHING, FATHER!" sobbed the distraught princess.

Princess Phlema remained curled up on the floor, a complete wreck. She sobbed and sobbed, just as anyone would if they had lost their goat.

"Does this mean our game is over?" Edwart inquired meekly.

The king wanted to grab Edwart's nose and twist it off. "Yes, it's over . . . and I won," he blurted.

"Your Majesty, excuse the intrusion," came a timid voice from the hallway. The king and the wizard looked up to see two monks standing bashfully in the doorway.

The two men wore the frocks and sash of the Green Order, the group of holy clerics charged with maintaining the ancient traditions of Boo'Gar and keeping guard over the priceless *Book of Loogey*.

"What are you two doing here?" questioned the king.

"Your Majesty," the shorter one said. "We have some troubling news to report." He was holding a piece of crumpled parchment.

The king looked at the parchment and held out his hand. "OK, let's have it."

The monks shuffled in sheepishly and handed the note to the king. As he read the note, his eyes darkened. His mouth drooped into a deep frown.

"A ransom!" shouted the king. "They want us to bring the sacred *Book of Loogey* into the forest and hand it over to them in exchange for Babycakes!"

Edwart the wizard gasped, "No, Your Greatness! We mustn't!"

The *Book of Loogey* was kept under lock and key in the North Tower of the castle. It contained a collection of mystical teachings, handed down by ancient gods, known as the Gazoon'Tites.

The super-colossal book was so dangerous that no one dared open it, for it was rumored to contain deadly magical spells, prehistoric symbols, and at least one outstanding oatmeal cookie recipe.

King Mewkus held up his key to the tower. "Boo'Gar has been the proud guardian of that book for eons! I will not be the king who loses it now. There must be some other way to get Babycakes back."

"Your Majesty?" said the taller of the monks. "Who is this Babycakes? Perhaps an important member of your inner circle?"

"It's a goat," said Edwart flatly.

"MY DEAREST!" screamed Princess Phlema, "WHAAAAAAAAAaaaaaaa!"

The wailing of the princess filled the small room. Everyone stood around uncomfortably. The king motioned the two monks closer to discuss options for what to do next. They huddled in, and Edwart spoke first.

"Your Highness, perhaps we could pay them cash instead?"

"Cash?" said the king. "You know as well as I do that Boo'Gar is a poor kingdom. We have no money!"

15

"Perhaps we could rescue Babycakes by force?" asked the king.

"With what army?" questioned Edwart. "Our people are meek and mild. Boo'Gar has been peaceful for over a generation."

"Is that supposed to be *my* fault?" snapped the king defensively.

The taller monk made a suggestion. "Uh, what if we just give them the book they're asking for?"

The king looked sourly at the two monks. "What are your names, you two?"

The tall one spoke up. "I'm Flik and this is Pik, Your Majesty."

The king squared his shoulders on the two monks. "Well, Pik and Flik, you of all people should realize the power of that book. With one spell, someone could wipe out an entire kingdom! That's why the honorable people of Boo'Gar were chosen to keep it safe."

The two monks looked at the floor, embarrassed.

"No," continued the king. "We go after our royal goat by force, and we get him back." The king stood straight and tall. "My kingdom does not make deals with goatnappers."

Princess Phlema, overhearing the conversation, leapt to her feet and tearfully hugged her father. "Oh, Daddy, you're the best!"

"Are you sure about this, Your Highness?" said Edwart. "You don't have much experience with warfare."

King Mewkus glared at Edwart. "That's quite enough, wizard! You haven't exactly been tearing it up in the magic department lately, either," he spat out sarcastically. "Can't you conjure up an army of skeleton monkeys or something helpful?"

Princess Phlema elbowed her way into the men's circle. "Look, while you guys stand around pulling each other's beards, my goat is out there in the wilderness, scared and thinking that I've deserted him." Tears welled up in her eyes again.

The group stood there awkwardly, trying to come up with a plan that would keep the princess from losing it again.

"The Knights of Boo'Gar!" Edwart suddenly shouted.

"The who of the what?"

"Your royal order of knights could get Babycakes back," said Edwart. "You were just a lad, My King. But they once saved the entire kingdom!"

Edwart put his hand on the king's shoulder. "When you were a boy fifty years ago, the knighthood was activated to protect the village from a series of savage attacks."

Princess Phlema looked interested. "Attacks from what?"

"Bees," said the wizard.

"Excuse me?" asked the princess.

"An infestation of bees," said Edwart. "They were quite aggressive. From then on, the knights were supposed to remain ready. All we have to do is call them."

"Yes, yes, I've heard the stories many times," said the king, looking exasperated. "They destroyed our cantaloupe fields with their insecticides and their tromping around. My father made me swear not to use those lunatics again, unless I was desperate."

"Is this not a desperate situation?"

The king thought for a moment and wondered if he should trust the honor of his kingdom to a band of unruly warriors.

Princess Phlema broke the silence. "What are we waiting for? I say we call these awesome Knights of Boo'Gar and go kick some kidnapper butt!"

This gave the king the resolve he needed. "OK, so . . . how do we call them? Is there a signal? How do we get in touch with these Knights of Boo'Gar?"

Pik, the shorter monk, spoke up quietly. "Sire, if I may—legends tell us that the accepted way to call knights is to use the bell in the old bell tower."

Flik elbowed his fellow monk forcefully.

"Ouch!"

"Yes, that's right," said Edwart. "The bell tower."

"You mean *my* bell tower?" puzzled the king. "Do we still have a bell up there? I thought it was filled with old boxes and exercise equipment."

Then Flik spoke up once more. "Or . . . perhaps we could just give them the book and call it a day. Just putting that out there."

The king looked at the monk, annoyed. "Flik, guarding that sacred text is the only thing Boo'Gar has left to be proud of, so give it a rest! This is a good plan. We'll ring the bell and see if any of these bee knights are left to come to our aid." The king looked resolved. "Yes, I like this plan. It's proactive."

The group exchanged meaningful looks, all nodding in agreement. They paused for a moment, savoring the excitement to come. Princess Phlema dried her tears with her sleeve.

"TO THE BELL TOWER!" she shouted.

With that, King Mewkus and his loyal wizard Edwart, Princess Phlema, and the two monks, Pik and Flik, went running out of the game room and up the dark stairs of the musty old bell tower.

Chapter 2

The heroic traditions of the Knights of Boo'Gar had faded over the many decades after the bee attacks. The knights did their best to keep up their training, but time is the enemy of tradition. Like everything else that was once great about the kingdom of Boo'Gar, the knights had fallen upon hard times.

Sir Malcolm was forced to sell his armor to pay off a debt. Sir Daphne gave up the knighthood to start her real estate business. Sir John became a tax attorney. And Sir Ralph started a chain of grocery stores.

So it was that young Sir Rowland, thirteen years of age and the lone surviving Knight of Boo'Gar, knelt in his garden on that fateful morning, turning the soil and humming his happy gardening tune.

"Hum, dum, laa day doo," sang Rowland as he pulled weeds out of his turnip beds. "Isn't today just the perfect weather, Angelina?"

Rowland's pet turtle, Angelina, sat warming herself in the sun and said nothing. She was only a turtle, but to a lonely Rowland she was more like a best friend.

"I think we might just spend the rest of our lives right here in this garden. Wouldn't that be marvelous, Angelina?"

A loud bell suddenly echoed across the valley.

Rowland looked up from his gardening.

"BOOOONNNNNGGGGGGGGGG!" A second time.

Rowland was confused.

"BOOOONNNNNGGGGGGGGGG!" A third time.

The echo faded and the valley fell silent. Rowland struggled to understand . . . to remember. "That bell," he said. "It means something."

Slowly, Rowland's eyes widened as he remembered his obligation. He remembered what the bell meant.

"BOOOONNNNNGGGGGGGGGG!"

Rowland jumped up, spraying dirt and turnip plants everywhere. Angelina tucked into her shell as Rowland started screaming, "THE BELL!" he screamed. "The Knight's Bell!"

"BOOOONNNNNGGGGGGGGGG!"

Rowland ran into his little hut, tearing off his gardening clothes as he went, hopping on one foot as he pulled off his farmer boots and getting tangled in his sweater as he struggled to take it off over his head.

"BOOOONNNNNGGGGGGGGGG!"

"Yes! I hear you!" said Rowland. "I'm coming!"

"BOOOONNNNNGGGGGGGGGG!"

"Angelina! Where is my armor?" gasped Rowland. He stumbled over some old plant crates and fell to the floor. "Owwwww!"

"BOOOONNNNNGGGGGGGGGG!"

Jumping up and tearing through his dresser drawers, throwing assorted items over his shoulder, Rowland frantically searched for his equipment. "Why now? Why now? Why now?" Rowland chanted as he launched clothing all over the room.

Angelina slowly made her way through the doorway and into the hut to watch her human go crazy. It was clear that she really liked the boy. Maybe it was his big feet or his snorting laugh.

"Ah-HAA!" squeaked Rowland, as he raised his leather tunic in the air in victory. "Found it!" he continued.

Rowland put on each piece of his uniform as he found it. A stocking, chain mail leggings, his right boot, a left glove . . . and before long, he was dressed.

Rowland went outside carrying his shoulder bag. He picked up his turtle. "Don't worry, Angelina. I could never leave my special friend behind."

He gently slipped the turtle into his pack. Then he called for his faithful ostrich, Tulip.

"Tuuuuuuulip! Time for an exciting adventure!" he called.

Tulip the ostrich trotted over from behind the shed. She nuzzled Rowland behind the ear, making him erupt in giggles and push her away.

"Ha-ha, stop it, you goof. We have to leave now to go serve our king. It's very important and exciting," he said with a serious tone.

Tulip was not sure about this. She much preferred the quiet farm life, and she could sense that Rowland was a little nervous. She squawked nervously as he climbed up onto her saddle with his bag and a few supplies. "Squawwwk," said Tulip.

"It'll be fun, Tulip. You'll see," said Rowland.

Rowland named her Tulip as a joke because, in fact, she didn't have any lips at all, not one lip or two lips. She was a bird. Rowland thought this was hilarious, but Tulip just liked being named after a flower.

Rowland switched to his deeper, serious voice to address his traveling companions. "Angelina. Tulip. We have been called into service as knights," said the boy. "The hour is at hand, and we're off on a dangerous adventure."

Angelina listened from inside her bag, and Tulip let out a honk to show that she was ready. "Honnnnk."

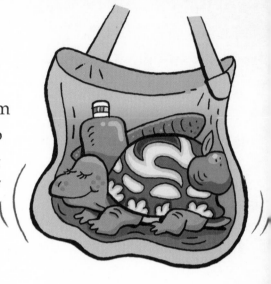

Rowland turned to look at his little farm one more time before trotting off in the direction of Castle Boo'Gar.

Chapter 3

In the castle courtyard, King Mewkus and Edwart had assembled the royal court to receive the Knights of Boo'Gar as they marched majestically through the gates. Brightly colored flags hung from the castle walls, and a small band of flutes and drums played the Mewkus family overture. It was a bouncy tune called "A Hasty Retreat."

34

The lords and ladies of the royal court had been advised of the tragic kidnapping, so they had gathered in their most solemn attire, their puffy red faces looking damp and concerned under a hot morning sun.

The king had changed into his formal crown, and Princess Phlema stood tall in her tiara, dressed in her favorite blue velvet jumper and wearing her favorite tool belt. She was the picture of composure now, and no one would ever guess that she'd been crying earlier. Now she stood proud and determined.

The two monks of the Green Order, Pik lingered behind the king and princess, weari stiff ceremonial robes. Pik nervously fingered the his sleeve.

Edwart the wizard stood calmly, his fingertips touching as he surveyed the festive scene, nodding to the assembled nobility and trying to look extra magical.

King Mewkus looked around the courtyard. It had been years since he'd felt so important and in charge. Perhaps this kidnapping was just the thing he needed to get his kingdom back on track and to start ruling like a king again—more like his father.

He pictured the scene to come. Perhaps five hundred knights would ride into the courtyard and bow to him. He'd say something inspirational and the crowd would cheer. It was going to be grand.

Perhaps he would lead the knights into battle against the evil kidnappers and ride back into the castle carrying Babycakes. His daughter would be so proud of him.

"A rider approaches!" shouted a teenage girl perched high up on the castle wall.

A ripple of movement went through the crowd as they moved toward the gate to see the gleaming armor of the imposing champions riding under their colorful banners. The atmosphere was charged with excitement, and everyone held their breath and waited for that moment—the moment they'd tell their grandchildren about.

Princess Phlema stood on tiptoes to see over the crowd. "Who is it? How many are there? How handsome are they on a scale from one to ten?" she bobbed her head to see. "Um, is that an ostrich?"

Sir Rowland rode alone through the gate to the triumphant blare of the royal trumpets. The Mewkus overture reached a thundering crescendo, which unfortunately spooked Rowland's timid ostrich. Tulip jumped back, throwing Rowland into the air and landing him in a coop full of chickens.

The royal court looked on in horror as chickens flew everywhere. Rowland's ostrich squawked and then pooped right in the courtyard.

"I'm fine. Not a problem!" shouted Sir Rowland from beneath twenty chickens. He jumped up, pulling feathers from his hair, and walked over to the king. The musicians stopped playing.

"Your Majesty!" Sir Rowland squeaked.

He pulled a small, tattered card out of his pocket and read aloud so that the crowd could hear him. "I am Sir Rowland Pockmyer, son of Rufus. I have come in answer to your call. How can the Knights of Boo'Gar assist you?"

Everyone stood in stunned silence. Princess Phlema frowned and looked back at the gate. King Mewkus plucked a chicken feather out of his teeth.

The wizard Edwart spoke up first. "Uh, good Sir Knight. Shouldn't we wait for the other knights to show up?"

Sir Rowland looked back at the gate, hopefully. "Umm, actually, I think I'm pretty much it, Your Wizardship."

More silence. Somewhere, a chicken squawked.

"You gotta be kidding me!" cried Princess Phlema. She turned to look at her father.

"Good Sir Rowland," asked the king. "Are there not hundreds of you under my command?"

Sir Rowland cleared his throat. "Actually—ahem—there's a funny story behind that. See, most of them have retired. I'm the only one left," said Rowland uncomfortably.

"What about Sir Winston?" asked Edwart.

"Oh, he started a weasel stand in Sneezix."

"I think I remember a Sir Justin?" asked the king.

"Yes, unfortunately Justin quit to start a boy band," said Rowland.

Princess Phlema stepped forward. "How old are you, kid?"

"I am almost fourteen, Your Ladyship."

The royals turned to look at each other. Edwart shrugged his shoulders. The princess crossed her arms and scowled. The king's dreams of leading a brave army evaporated before his eyes as he looked Rowland up and down.

King Mewkus thought to himself, "Has my kingdom finally come to this? A thirteen-year-old ragamuffin is my only knight?"

The king sighed. "Well, perhaps I should bring you up to speed on the situation then," he said with solemn emphasis. "You see, there's been a kidnapping."

"A what?" said Sir Rowland.

"A kidnapping," said the king. "One of our royal goats has been taken."

"And you think bees are responsible?"

"Bees? No, no—a person took the goat. It's a kidnapping," said the king with irritation. "Didn't you hear me?"

"Oh . . . I see, well," said Rowland slowly. "We mostly deal with bees. At least, that's what I was trained for."

"You mean all you do is practice battling bees all day?" asked the wizard.

Rowland continued with confidence. "Yes, it made sense since that's what we were asked to do last time. We developed a number of very effective . . ."

"Look, this doesn't have anything to do with bees, you silly child!" interrupted Princess Phlema. "My goat has been taken, and we need you to go get it back," she cried. " And kick someone's behind. You guys are supposed to be so terrifying and efficient."

"Your Highness," called Pik the monk. "This young boy can't possibly hope to rescue a goat from dangerous captors all by himself."

"I was actually going to say the same thing," said Rowland. "I have no weapons. Only my bee-handling equipment," he continued. "Perhaps I could use one of my nets to . . ."

"Will you drop the bee thing?" shouted Phlema. "There are no bees!"

The king tried to diffuse the situation. "Look, everyone, calm down, OK? Can you at least look into this kidnapping for us? We'd really appreciate it."

Suddenly, the wizard turned around and thoughtfully walked back toward the castle door. The king called out to him.

"Where are you going, Edwart?" he asked.

"I have an idea," said Edwart. "I'll be right back."

The king turned back to Rowland. "We received this note. We need you to venture into the forest and track down these kidnappers. Can you at least try?" He handed the note to Rowland.

Sir Rowland looked at the note, then at Princess Phlema. Her lip trembled with emotion again. She feared she would never see her lovely Babycakes ever again. It was all too much.

Sir Rowland felt a surge of bravery. "I will do my best, Your Majesty. It will be my honor to track down these bees . . . uh . . . I mean these kidnappers."

He paused in thought. "Are they called kidnappers because baby goats are called kids?"

The king looked at him like he was crazy. "No! They are called kidnappers because they abducted someone against their will. Look, are you sure you're up for this?"

Some of the nobles in the crowd exchanged concerned glances.

"Ah, of course. Yes, Your Majesty. This will be a piece of cake. Yes," stammered Rowland.

The wizard returned to the group carrying a long object covered in fine green velvet. He stopped in front of Sir Rowland and, with great ceremony, unwrapped the object.

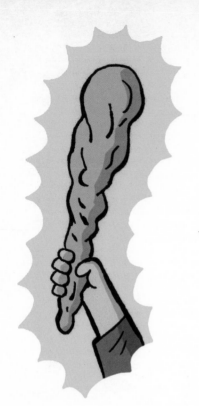

"Good Sir Rowland," intoned Edwart. "May I present to you your weapon. Passed down through generations of wizards. Enchanted by the elves of Highmark, and blessed by the friars of Vallejo. I present to you the Staff of Slumber."

The crowd of lords and ladies recoiled with a gasp.

"Jiminy jaguars," whispered Princess Phlema.

The wizard held out a long, gnarled wooden shaft to Rowland. Rowland took the staff and looked at it. The wood had a blue-green tint to it. It was carved from top to bottom with ancient symbols, and it felt very heavy and well balanced in his hands. Rowland thought he felt a tingle run through his fingers.

"This will make a fine weapon. Thank you, wizard."

"Use it wisely, good knight," said Edwart. "For the Staff of Slumber has great power. All who are touched by its magic will fall into a deep, dreamless sleep."

"Cool," said Sir Rowland. He held the staff in both hands, making swiping gestures right and left to get the feel of it.

The princess thought he looked rather knightly after all.

With this, the crowd of lords and ladies erupted in a loud cheer.

"Hooray!" said the crowd.

The band struck up the Mewkus overture again. Three maidens came out of the crowd and threw rose petals on Rowland, and the king and his court clapped enthusiastically.

"Well then," smiled the king. "It looks like we have our champion after all. Good luck, Sir Rowland!"

Tulip was led into the center of the courtyard wearing a finely crafted new saddle. It was packed with a mountain of fresh supplies. Rowland took his new weapon and climbed up onto the saddle. He looked down at the stable boy holding the reins.

"Uh, sorry about the mess," said Sir Rowland.

Everyone glanced down at the "deposit" that Tulip had left on the ground. The lords and ladies held lace hankies to their nose. Tulip blushed a deep red.

The monks, Pik and Flik, approached Rowland and called up to him. "Start your search in the Dark Woods."

"I will do as you say," Rowland replied. He gave the princess a self-assured look and raised one eyebrow for effect. The princess looked at him and shrugged.

With that, Sir Rowland turned Tulip around and headed out the gates of Castle Boo'Gar to the cheers of a grateful crowd. The band played joyously, and Tulip walked with extra snap in her stride as they marched off into their first great adventure.

"Yo! Sir Rowland!" cried Princess Phlema. "Bring me back my goat!"

The princess then tossed him a single white rose. It floated through the air to the brave knight, rolling against a cruel blue sky. Time seemed to slow down as Rowland reached . . . out . . . to . . . grab . . . it . . . and . . . he totally missed.

There was an audible groan of disappointment from the crowd, as the rose landed in the mud in front of the gate. Rowland chose not to see this as a bad omen and waved enthusiastically to the crowd.

King Mewkus took a step closer to his trusted wizard. "We are in deep doo-doo," muttered the king.

Chapter 4

Rowland rode into the valley of Boo'Gar under a warm afternoon sun. The three kingdoms that made up the land of Loogey stretched out before him. He wondered how far his quest might take him.

To the north lay the wealthy province of Sneezix, a kingdom made famous for its gold and for having the last remaining Handsome Tree in existence.

It was well known that anyone who consumed the fruit of the enchanted Handsome Tree would be granted a life of beauty and grace. King Sinius, the young ruler of Sneezix, proudly displayed the tree in front of his stately gleaming white castle. It was a sight that Rowland had always wanted to see.

Druél

Sneezix

Boo'Gar

N

To the northwest lay the rugged, rocky land of Druél. A ruthless soldier named Lord Cassius Znott led the brutal warriors of that kingdom. No one dared to set foot into Druél without expecting a fight. The Drooligans, as they were called, were known for having quick tempers and a great enthusiasm for sharp blades.

Boo'Gar, by comparison, had only the *Book of Loogey* to be proud of. They had no magic tree or vaults filled with gold, like Sneezix. They had no skill on the battlefield like Druél, and the only crops they could grow successfully were turnips. The people of Boo'Gar were known to be simple, plain-looking folks of few talents, and poor King Mewkus was no exception.

None of that mattered to Rowland as he bumped along. He loved his king, and he was proud to be riding into battle to honor him, even if it was a little scary . . . and uncomfortable. The new leather saddle that Rowland had received for Tulip was chaffing his bottom a bit.

"Snots, Tulip. Is this saddle hurting you as much as it is me?"

"Honk!" said Tulip.

SNEEZIX   **DRUÉL**   **BOO'GAR**

Rowland kept a steady pace for hours, riding through small villages and past humble inns on his way to the Dark Woods. Farmers and shopkeepers went about their afternoon tasks, unaware of his important mission.

He passed a group of women shampooing a wildebeest for some reason. In the village square, an old man sat on the front steps of the meeting hall weaving a pair of shoes out of turnip leaves. Rowland rode up to the man.

"Good afternoon, sir," said Rowland. "Can you show me the way to the Dark Woods?"

The startled man looked up from his project and squinted at the young knight.

56

"We don't have any dark woods. You must be lost."

Rowland thought for a minute. "Do you have woods of any kind? They might not be dark. Maybe just shady?" he asked hopefully.

The man looked annoyed. "So you're changing your story now? You tourists are all alike."

Rowland sat up tall in the saddle. "Sir, I'm a knight of King Mewkus. I'm traveling to the Dark Woods to rescue a . . ."

"We have a forest, but no woods," said the distracted villager. "Looks like you're out of luck."

The old man spat and went back to his weaving.

"No, a forest is good!" said Rowland. "Lots of tress packed tightly together? Which way do I go for that?"

The old man didn't look up from his project. He simply pointed down the street with his thumb. "Follow Muddley Lane, then turn left at Dark Woods Road. That will lead you to the forest."

"So . . . the road is called Dark Woods Road?" asked Rowland patiently.

"Yes," said the man. "What about it?"

"Oh, nothing," said Rowland. "Thanks so much for your help."

"Do you want to buy a pair of turnip leaf shoes?" asked the man, suddenly hopeful.

"Um, not today, thank you," said Rowland. "You've been of great help, citizen. The king thanks you."

"Whatever," said the man. "I hate tourists."

Soon Rowland
found Dark Woods
Road and followed
it out of the village,
through some fields
and up to the edge of
the forest. It was late
afternoon and a tangerine
sun hung low in the sky.
Rowland felt a chilly breeze
against the back of his neck as he gave a
light kick to guide Tulip into the murky shadows
between the trees.

He discovered a modest path to a trail, deeply
carpeted in soft pine needles. As the trail narrowed, tree
branches snatched at Rowland's shoulders. He felt another
chill across his neck.

Nightfall settled around Rowland, Tulip, and Angelina.
The forest came alive with the sounds
of crickets and frogs . . . and then
suddenly Rowland heard what
sounded like an owl being hit
with an accordion. The young
knight jumped.

Rowland stopped on the path to let his nerves settle. He decided to check on Angelina, so he removed the turtle from his bag and gently held her up to his face, nose to nose.

"Hello, brave Angelina. You aren't afraid, are you?" said Rowland with a slight tremor to his voice. In the dim light, he could just make out Angelina looking back at him and blinking.

"Shall we press deeper into this forest, Angelina?" Rowland asked. "Or perhaps it's best to head back to the village, maybe get a room for the night? How does that sound?" Rowland knew in his heart that this was a cowardly option.

"That's a long walk back, you cowardly slump-shouldered puffball," came a gruff reply.

Rowland sat there for a moment, confused. "Did my turtle just call me a puffball?" he thought.

"YOU!" came a shout from the bushes. "Off the horse, now! And hand over that turtle."

Rowland whirled around in the direction of the voice. He peered deeply into the woods. It was a terrible voice filled with hate and broken dreams. Rowland thought he could see the outline of a huge distorted figure. Perhaps it was a bear . . . or a very large monkey. Maybe even a bear dressed as a monkey. Whatever it was, it was moving toward him from the inky darkness.

"Halt!" cried Sir Rowland in a high-pitched voice. "In the name of His Highness, King Mewkus! I am Rowland, a Knight of Boo'Gar. You will let me pass!"

There was quiet.

Then slowly a low chuckle bubbled up through the dark. "Hee-hee-hee," chuckled the creature. "A Knight of Boo'Gar, he says. HA-HA-HA-HA-HA-HA-HA-HA-HA-HA-HA!"

The creature stepped into a shaft of dappled moonlight, and Rowland could see that it was merely a man—a very large ugly man, but a man nevertheless. He was covered in dirt and completely bald, with a twisted misshapen nose and yellow eyes. He wore a faded battle shirt stained with blood and taco sauce. A rusty old axe was tucked into a leather belt cinched around his wide belly.

As the man approached, Rowland suddenly caught a whiff of his pungent smell.

"I'm still going to steal all your stuff, boy. I don't care what you are," said the smelly man. "Off the horse . . . now."

Rowland remained on Tulip, who was clearly not a horse. He sat up extra tall, trying to look more imposing. His hand slowly moved to the Staff of Slumber.

"Good sir, I am on a vital mission for King Mewkus. It will not go well for you if you keep me from my task," said Rowland, working hard to keep the squeak out of his voice.

The stranger peered at Rowland for a moment, his eyes narrowing. "Have the bees returned to Boo'Gar?" questioned the stranger.

Rowland looked surprised. "Uh, excuse me? How did you . . . ?"

The stranger was quiet. Suddenly his eyes came alive in a crazy way. "Contain and transport—wasn't that the method for dealing with bees?"

Rowland's jaw dropped. "Good sir, how did you know . . . ?"

The stranger spoke again. "Sir Crustos is my name. Of course, I've been retired for a while, but I still remember the Knights' Creed."

He cleared his throat dramatically and began, "We are the Knights of Boo'Gar."

Rowland's face lit up, and they continued the chant together.

"When trouble's here, we will be there.

"In dark of night, in cold of gloom.

"Shedding light, dispelling doom."

Rowland smiled wide and hopped down from his saddle. His legs were stiff from the long ride, causing him to walk like a rubber cowboy.

"Good Sir Crustos, it is a relief to meet a brother in this bleak forest. I was afraid my ostrich was getting frightened."

Sir Crustos's lips curled back in a wide grin, revealing yellow teeth. "Right. Your ostrich, hee-hee." Crustos softened and approached Rowland to shake his hand.

"I'll tell you what, boy," he said. "I have a fire going at my camp. Let's roast that turtle of yours to make a nice pot of soup. I have some brown bread. It will be a feast."

Rowland was still cradling Angelina in his arms. The old knight approached, but stopped short when he saw the turtle's shell up close. Crustos stumbled back, a look of shock on his face.

"I have a better idea," said Rowland, changing the subject. "The king has given me gold, weapons, and enough food for a week's journey. If you join my quest, fellow knight, half of it will be yours, and we can eat the delicious food that King Mewkus has given me."

Sir Crustos regained his composure. He thought for a moment. "More food, huh? And gold, you say?"

In fact, there was no gold, but Rowland had decided to add that for emphasis. "Oh yes, I'm loaded down with money and enough castle food for a real feast."

The old knight threw his head back and let out a howl of laughter, "WHAAA-HAA-HAW-HAW-HAW!"

"You've got yourself a deal, boy-oh!" said Crustos. "I'll take the food and half the prize money! Sounds like a good deal for old Crustos."

The two knights shook hands. Rowland was very thankful to be wearing thick, clean gloves.

"On one condition," interrupted Sir Crustos. "After this is all over, I still want that turtle of yours, for a pet. Do we have a deal?"

Rowland panicked. "Uh, sounds good, sir knight. We have a deal."

Rowland knew that Angelina was looking at him with her sweet, trusting eyes. He felt like a traitor.

With the partnership formed, and Crustos officially unretired as a knight, Rowland and Tulip were led through a small opening in a blackberry thicket, and onto a narrow, lumpy path that led to Crustos's hidden camp.

There was a fresh campfire crackling and popping next to a giant hollowed-out tree trunk that the old knight was using for shelter.

Rowland looked around with a curdled expression on his face. "You live in a rotten tree?"

"All the comforts of home, Reggie!" said Sir Crustos cheerfully. "You're a real knight now. You have to make do with what you find."

"It's Rowland, sir."

Rowland was still not sure about the strange knight, but he was happy to have some company at last.

The chill of nighttime closed in, and a smoky blue moon watched them from high above the trees. The young knight unpacked the food from Tulip's saddle.

Later, sitting close to the warm fire, Rowland happily munched on bacon and hard cheese, and told Crustos all about Babycakes and the kidnappers. Crustos nodded and grunted as Rowland told the story.

When Rowland was finished, the two sat in silence.

Finally Crustos spoke. "You know, Boo'Gar was once a much more powerful kingdom. There were cantaloupe fields for as far as you could see. And the castle had lots of money back then, too. I remember King Mewkus's father."

Crustos picked up his rusty old axe and examined it wistfully. He had a sad look in his eyes. Then, as if to change the subject . . .

"I once had fourteen bees in my pants," said the knight brightly. "I was right there in the middle of that famous bee invasion. I had to run for miles and jump into a lake!" He set his axe down and leaned back, picking his teeth.

Crustos abruptly leaned to one side, and let go with a powerful blast of gas. FIRRRT! "Thar she blows!" the excited knight said with a laugh.

After a time, the forest grew quiet. Rowland finished eating and leaned back against a soft log. He tugged his blanket up around himself and around Angelina, still feeling a little guilty about agreeing to pass her off to Crustos.

Angelina didn't seem to be holding a grudge, as she cuddled up next to her boy, sound asleep.

Chapter 5

The next morning, Rowland awakened to find Crustos studying a faded map painted onto worn leather. Tulip had been fed and packed up. The fire was out and everything seemed ready to go.

"Ahhh, Prince Lazybones is finally awake," teased Sir Crustos. "So as I understand it, we're looking for a stolen goat. And we're not quite sure where to look. Is that correct?"

"That is the situation, Sir Crustos," said Rowland.

"Well, you're in luck, boy," said Crustos. "I happen to have an enchanted object that will lead us right to your precious goat. Have you ever heard of an Orb of Seeing?" asked the old knight.

Rowland shrugged and shook his head. Crustos pulled a round, smooth crystal out of his pack and held it up to the morning sunlight. Rowland had never seen anything like it.

"I got this from some traveling merchants yesterday," said Crustos. "I traded it for my only bar of soap."

Rowland was pretty sure that Crustos needed soap more than a dumb-looking glass ball.

The orb was a foggy white color with flecks of orange and green. Rowland could almost see through it, but the sunlight caused the center to glow and churn like angry clouds. Crustos peered into the device intensely.

"Come look at this, Rowland," said Crustos, motioning Rowland over.

Rowland stood shoulder to shoulder with the smelly old knight and squinted into the orb. To his astonishment, a little moving picture started to form.

"I think that's Babycakes!" shouted Rowland excitedly. "It looks like he's tied up in some sort of cave."

A little movie was playing inside the enchanted orb, and Rowland could make out a dark cave with a frightened goat shivering in the gloom. A heavy chain was hanging around his neck. "Poor Babycakes," thought Rowland.

"I think I recognize that cave," whispered Crustos. "There's an entrance near the Cliffs of Boo'Gar, farther north. I bet the Nose Goblins who live in those caves have your goat."

"Nose Goblins?" squeaked Rowland nervously. "That doesn't sound good. What's a Nose Goblin?"

"Oh, just terrifying ogres with runny noses who are twelve feet tall, and like to eat people for dinner," said the old knight casually.

Rowland suddenly felt a little sick.

"But that's not the worst part," added Crustos. "To get to those caves, we'll have to travel through some very nasty territory. We probably won't even make it to the caves alive . . . so that's a bummer."

Rowland swallowed hard.

Rowland was on a quest, and he knew that being on a quest sometimes involved taking risks, including getting killed and eaten in all sorts of violent, unpleasant ways. Once you choose the path of a brave knight, you have to expect things to get a little dicey.

Rowland pictured Princess Phlema's flawless face. His heart did a little flip-flop.

The last of the supplies were packed and Crustos was ready to go. "I don't have a horse of my own," said Crustos. "So we'll ride together on your horse. She looks pretty strong."

"Are you serious?" squawked Rowland. "First of all, she's an ostrich, not a horse! And she can barely carry all my stuff and me. What happened to your horse?"

Crustos rubbed his whiskers and looked down. "Well . . . uh, I was out here a long time. I got pretty hungry and . . ."

"Never mind! I don't want to know," said Rowland flatly.

"Tasted worse than shoe leather," muttered Crustos. "Anyway, we're wasting time," he said, changing the subject.

He opened his map for Rowland. "We'll travel north, through Itchy Plant Lagoon," said Crustos. "Up the trail through the Boogerbald Mountains, and then the worst part . . . through the Arachni Valley, otherwise known as the Valley of Spiders."

Rowland looked at Crustos. "Valley of . . . ?"

"Spiders, yes," said Crustos.

Tulip the ostrich let out a high-pitched whine. "Eeeeep."

Rowland reluctantly climbed up onto Tulip's saddle. Her thin legs shook as the extra-large Crustos stepped up onto a tree stump, and then hopped up onto the ostrich.

"Oooff!" said Tulip. Her legs strained to hold the weight.

With everyone aboard, Tulip took the first shaky step of the long journey ahead. Rowland thought about the bravery of his sweet ostrich. He patted her soft back, and then he checked his shoulder bag to make sure Angelina was still safe.

She looked up at him and blinked her trusting eyes. She was an excellent turtle.

"Next stop: Itchy Plant Lagoon!" shouted Crustos. For emphasis, he leaned up in the saddle and passed gas. FIRRRT! "Thar she blows!"

Chapter 6

The same sun that bathed Rowland and Crustos in warm morning light also shone down upon Castle Boo'Gar, many miles away.

Deep inside the castle, far beyond the reach of even the most persistent sunbeam, darkness was gathering. There, in the dungeons where the Green Order of monks hold their secret ceremonies, Pik stood next to Babycakes, stirring fresh blueberries into his oatmeal. The royal goat was known to be a picky eater, and Pik didn't want to be accused of starving the missing animal.

"There you go, darling, a perfect recipe," said Pik. He spooned the fruity glop into Babycakes's bowl. The little goat looked at the bowl and reluctantly began to eat. At first, Babycakes only plucked the sweet berries out, one by one. Soon he was taking big hungry bites and eating happily.

"Pik, get over here," hissed Flik. "We're about to dial King Sinius."

Flik was sitting at a sturdy oak table. In the middle of the table was a small cauldron of bubbling liquid. Flik held a glass tube of green goop just above the cauldron. Pik pulled a heavy chair up to the table and sat down.

Flik dripped a few drops of green goop into the cauldron. FOOM! A shaft of green light exploded out of the cauldron and projected an image onto the ceiling above the table.

"Hello? King Sinius?" called Flik. "Are you there, sir? Hello?"

Pik and Flik waited for a response, trading a nervous glance. The picture on the ceiling fluttered and came to life. A three-dimensional image of King Sinius on his throne suddenly floated above the cauldron.

"Hello, is that you, King Sinius?" called Flik.

Young King Sinius appeared to be talking rapidly, but the two monks heard no sound. Flik moved the cauldron a little.

"King Sinius! We can't hear you!" yelled Flik. "There's a problem with the sound!"

The frustrated king then reached out to adjust the cauldron on his end. "Hello . . . doesn't . . . can't . . . thing." That was all the monks could make out.

"Wait, let me try something!" yelled Flik, hopefully.

He put another drop of goop into the cauldron and moved it a little to the left. The picture abruptly cut off, but the king's voice abruptly filled the room.

"...DARN THING NEVER WORKS!"

"Uh, King Sinius, we can hear you now! Can you hear us?" asked Flik sheepishly.

"Yes, I can hear you now, but I have no picture!" snapped the king.

"Sorry, sir. We might have to just get by with voices. My tele-cauldron seems to be acting up."

"Fine. I don't have all day. I'm a busy king. Now, did you get the *Book of Loogey* for me?"

"Uh, about that, Your Lordship," said Flik. "It seems that King Mewkus has dispatched a knight to rescue the goat."

"What?" squawked an agitated King Sinius. "You nimrods had a simple job! Kidnap the goat and force the king to hand over that book! Who are these knights?"

"The Knights of Boo'Gar, Your Lordship," said Pik. "We had forgotten about them, too. Apparently one of them still exists, but he's just a dim-witted boy. Nothing to worry about."

Flik interrupted his brother monk. "We've already taken care of it, My Lord," said Flik. "He won't be a problem."

King Sinius didn't seem convinced. "I don't want any complications, do you hear me?" he growled. "After I have that book in my possession, Sneezix will be the most powerful kingdom in all of Loogey!"

"And Pik and I will be given castles and gold, right, Your Lordship?" Flik asked pointedly.

"Sure, sure. You'll get something good," said Sinius impatiently. "But, remember, you'll also need the key around Mewkus's neck. Otherwise you can't get into the tower. Understand?"

"Yes, My Evil Lord," stammered Flik.

"Hee-hee, 'Evil Lord,' I like that," snarled King Sinius. "This is going to be great. I'm going to enjoy having all the power." Then he let out a creepy laugh.

"Mwah-ha-ha-ha. Wha-ha-ha-ha!"

Flik tried to match his evil laugh. "Whoo-ha-hee-hee."

"Stop that at once!" screamed King Sinius. "You sound ridiculous. You're not even doing it right."

Sinius paused, and then asked quietly, "What about Princess Phlema?" he asked. "Does she ever talk about me?"

Pik and Flik shifted uneasily in their chairs.

Sinius continued. "Do you know what kind of music she listens to? I want to make her a playlist."

"Uh, we should probably be getting back to our shadowy scheming," said Flik.

Sinius sounded disappointed. He dismissed them with a tired wave of his hand. "Oh, yes, don't let me keep you from your dumb ceremonies and cookies. By all means, carry on."

"Good-bye, King Sinius," said Flik.

Pik covered the tele-cauldron with a heavy cloth. The sound sputtered and then faded out completely. The two monks sat in silence.

"Well, that could have gone a lot worse," said Flik happily. "Isn't this exciting? Once King Mewkus gives us the book in exchange for Babycakes, we'll become heroes in the land of Sneezix. We'll never have to wear these dumb robes, or sing, or light candles again. We can wear fine silks and slip-on shoes. We'll have servants . . . and maybe even get skateboards!"

"You've always wanted a skateboard," said Pik sadly. "All of this sneaking around makes me nervous. We're the ones who will get thrown in jail if we get caught, not King Sinius. Besides," he added softly, "I don't like being the bad guy."

"Stop worrying, Pik. We'll move the goat to someplace safe, and as long as King Mewkus doesn't know that we're behind the plan, it can't fail."

Pik didn't seem convinced. He scratched Babycakes behind the ears and watched the sweet little goat finish his oatmeal.

"He's kind of a cute little guy," said Pik.

"Who, that goat?" said Flik. "He reminds me of my uncle Larry."

"Nyaaaaaaaa," said Babycakes.

Chapter 7

Rowland and Crustos exploded out of the jungle, exhausted from the trials of Itchy Plant Lagoon and Spider Valley. They collapsed onto the soft grass just beyond the jungle, panting and wheezing.

"Well," gasped a worn-out Crustos, "that'll be something to tell your grandchildren about, boy."

The long journey had been just as difficult as Crustos had warned, and the brave knights were almost dead from exhaustion.

Rowland lay on his back, panting. He turned to his fellow knight.

"Should I leave out the part—pant, pant—where you ran, screaming like a baby, and left me to beat off those things with my Staff of Slumber?" Rowland brushed a tiny spider off his shoulder.

"Yes, about that," said Crustos. "I didn't see you put any spiders to sleep. Are you sure that thing even works?"

"Of course the Staff of Slumber works," Rowland said angrily. "But not on tiny creatures. I thought the Valley of Spiders was going to be filled with giant spiders."

Crustos looked at Rowland. "Why would you assume such a thing? Spiders are very small. Everyone knows that."

"Listen," Rowland said. He leaned up on one elbow and looked at the knight. "We need to be more clear with our communication. I was ready for six, maybe seven humongous spiders, but not fifty million of the little creeps crawling all over us!" Rowland was still brushing at his clothes. "I was seriously freaked out, man."

Crustos smiled and scoffed. "Heh . . . I thought knights were supposed to have nerves of steel."

Rowland stood and brushed the dust off his shirt.

"Yeah, I saw your nerves of steel as you were running away."

STRETCH

CRAK!

Crustos stood and stretched. Rowland checked to see if Tulip and all of their gear had made it safely out of the jungle. The poor ostrich lay a few feet away, frazzled and breathing hard. Her legs were covered in sticky spiderwebs. Rowland went to her.

"There, there now, sweet Tulip," he said softly. "Everything's going to be OK. There are no more spiders."

Rowland gently helped her to her feet, and then took her reins to lead her over to a shady spot beside a small stream. He felt a little guilty for bringing her on such a dangerous quest. She was a sweet farm ostrich and didn't belong out here in the wilderness.

"Why do you pamper that animal so?" growled Crustos. "I've never seen such a spoiled horse."

"You stay here and rest, Tulip," Rowland said quietly, patting her soft neck. "Never mind what the big smelly man says. We're going to explore a cave now, but you just relax."

Rowland found some ripened cantaloupes growing on vines next to the stream. He used a small knife to cut one in half for Tulip. The young knight scooped out the sweet orange center for her and this seemed to raise her spirits considerably. She munched happily on the juicy goodness.

"What in blazes are you doing, boy?" bellowed Crustos. "Do you know how much that cantaloupe would fetch in the city?"

Rowland ignored the salty old knight, but he did notice that the cantaloupe vines seemed to stretch for miles in both directions. He saw hundreds, probably thousands, of cantaloupes.

"Wow," puzzled Rowland. "I wonder if King Mewkus knows about all the cantaloupes growing out here in the wild?"

"Of course he does," reasoned Crustos. "You don't get to be king by missing something this obvious in your own kingdom!"

Rowland took a bite of sweet cantaloupe. The juice ran down his chin. "We're doing pretty well so far, aren't we, Crustos?"

For the first time, Rowland was starting to feel like a real knight on a true adventure. He handed a big chunk of fruit to Crustos, and the old knight made a huge mess of eating it.

"Well—munch, slurp—we aren't dead yet. That's something."

Rowland turned to look up at the steep cliffs looming overhead. The Cliffs of Boo'Gar rose two hundred feet in the air. Solid white marble, shot through with red and orange streaks.

The wall of rock looked to Rowland like a giant mountain of ice cream dripping with strawberry sauce. The cantaloupe had piqued his appetite. He licked his lips hungrily.

"Here it is, young one," intoned Crustos solemnly as he walked up behind Rowland. "The legendary Cliffs of Boo'Gar."

"They look delicious."

"You're a strange kid, Rowland," said Crustos as he wiped his juice-covered hands across his shirt.

Rowland shrugged. He squinted up at the high cliffs. "So, what's at the very top? Have you ever been up there?"

"That's the Kingdom of Druél," said Crustos. "We won't be going there. Not if we want to keep our heads."

"Oh, yes," said Rowland, cheerfully. "The first kingdom in all of Loogey."

Crustos ignored the comment. He didn't want to talk about Druél, so Rowland changed the subject.

"OK, so the Nose Goblins live inside these caves, right? How do we get in?"

Crustos touched Rowland's shoulder and pointed to the base of the cliff. "Look there, boy."

There was a huge stone disk hidden in the vines. It was twenty feet high and had ancient writing carved into its face. "What does it say?" asked Rowland.

"Uh, it says 'All who enter this cave, face certain death.'"

"CERTAIN DEATH?!" Rowland gulped.

"Either 'certain death' or 'silly dance,'" said Crustos. "I was never very good at reading Gazoon'Tite."

"I wish you had studied harder," gasped Rowland.

"Come on," said Crustos casually. "Let's get that stone rolled out of the way so we can get into that cave."

Looking at the stone, Rowland brightened. "Well, that shouldn't be too hard. It's round like a big wheel. We'll just give it a shove."

The two knights walked up to the two-ton stone. Crustos gave it a few hard pushes. It didn't budge. "This might be a little harder than you think, boy," said the old knight grimly.

Crustos directed Rowland to come stand beside him and lean into the stone. The old knight counted them off. "OK . . . one, two . . . three!"

"PUSH!" shouted Crustos.

"Ghaaaaaa, HOLY MAMA LLAMA!" shouted Rowland.

The stone didn't budge. They stopped pushing and stood with their hands on their knees, panting.

Suddenly, Crustos plunged his finger deep into his nose and started rooting around.

Rowland was a little shocked, "Uh, Sir Crustos, you're kind of grossing me out right now."

"Nose drippings!" shouted Crustos. "We'll use our nose drippings to grease the stone. Then it will slide away easily."

Crustos wiped his snot all along the edge of the large stone. Then he looked at Rowland. "Don't just stand there, boy. We'll need your nose drippings, too!"

Rowland looked over at Tulip, who stood watching them and had completely stopped eating her cantaloupe. Rowland shrugged his shoulders and rammed his finger up his own nose.

After they had both wiped down the stone with a generous amount of knight snot, they gave it another try. Crustos counted them off again. "OK . . . one, two . . . three!"

"PUSH!" shouted Crustos.

"HOLY MAMA LLAMA!" shouted Rowland.

This time the stone made a low grinding sound, and slowly started to roll. Krrrreeeeech!

"It's working!" shouted Rowland.

"PUSH!" screamed Crustos.

The ancient stone rolled thunderously out of the way, revealing a deep, dark cave. The two knights fell to the ground, exhausted.

"That was awesome!" gasped Rowland. "Woo-hoo!"

Crustos held up his hand. "Now remember, boy," he said with a steady, fatherly tone. "Picking your nose is only appropriate in certain situations. It's not something you do all the time."

Rowland smiled. "Oh, you mean it's sort of like farting and shouting, 'Thar she blows'?"

A wide grin cracked across Crustos's face. The two shared a lighthearted chuckle. "Hee-hee-hee-hee."

The Knights of Boo'Gar stood proudly before the dark jagged opening in the rocks. A cool, moist breeze blew from deep inside the cave, giving Rowland a sudden chill. Looking down into the gloom, he thought about the unknown terrors that might lie deep within.

Chapter 8

In Castle Boo'Gar, King Mewkus paced back and forth in his private chambers. The accounting books of the kingdom were strewn across a heavy wooden table, and the old king fiddled with the tower key that hung around his neck. It had been several days since he had sent poor Sir Rowland on his quest.

"Maybe I should have sent more men with him," Mewkus muttered to himself. "The inexperienced lad has probably been eaten by now, and Babycakes is still missing." The king knew he was running out of options.

Edwart stepped quietly into the king's chambers carrying a tray.

"Uh, I'm sorry to disturb you, Your Highness," said the wizard timidly. "I thought you might like a hot cup of turnip tea."

"Come in, Edwart. I'm always happy to see an old friend," said the king, patting the wizard on the shoulder.

The two men stood looking at the ledgers and accounting books.

"What's all this?" asked Edwart.

"Just checking the bank accounts one more time," said the king. "If only we had the money to pay for the return of Babycakes, this would all be over."

"It is just a goat, Your Highness," reasoned the wizard. "Perhaps . . ."

"No," said King Mewkus. "It's much more than a goat now. Boo'Gar is already the laughingstock of the land. My little girl is counting on me to fix this." The king's voice trembled with emotion. "There has to be a way."

Edwart looked concerned. "It's true. The poor princess has been distraught since her goat was taken. She's been cooped up in her workroom, fixing that old cantaloupe harvester," said Edwart. "I've never seen her so determined."

"The robot harvester?" questioned the king. "What could she be thinking?"

"I haven't a clue," Edwart said softly. "I was surprised that you let her take off by herself this morning, considering the emotional state she's been in."

"What?" the king blurted. "She took the harvester out? I gave no such permission. When did this happen?!"

Edwart fumbled. "Uh, well. She took some things from my lab and left about thirty minutes ago. She said she had your blessing, My King." The wizard stuttered defensively.

"WELL, SHE DIDN'T!" screamed the king. "You infernal fool. She's gone off to rescue that goat herself! Find those monks, Pik and Flik! We've got to get her back before she gets herself killed . . . or eaten . . . or worse!"

The two men ran out of the room, down the stairs, and through the courtyard leading to the monks' basement chambers. Then, suddenly . . .

"Oooff!"

They crashed right into the two monks as they were struggling up the steps, carrying a large bundle covered with a blanket.

"You two!" screamed the king. "My dear Phlema has gone off to rescue Babycakes herself. We have to find her!"

Pik and Flik looked at each other nervously. The bundle Flik was carrying was moving.

"Nyyaaaaa!" said the bundle.

Edwart looked down. There were four legs sticking out at the bottom. "Uh, what's that you're carrying, Flik?"

"Oh this? It's nothing," said Flik.

"It's our laundry," said Pik.

"Nyyaaaaa!" said the laundry.

For a brief moment, the four men looked at each other, then . . .

"RUN!" said Flik.

The monks shoved past Edwart and the king. The king felt a tug around his neck as Flik knocked him to the side.

"They're headed for the tower!" screamed King Mewkus. "They took my key! They're after the *Book of Loogey*! Stop them, Edwart."

The wizard knew just what to do. He stopped, planted his feet firmly, and took out his magical wand.

"A freeze spell should do the trick!" shouted Edwart with confidence.

He jabbed at the air with his wand and said the magic phrase he used for all his best spells, "Zooga-zallawalla!"

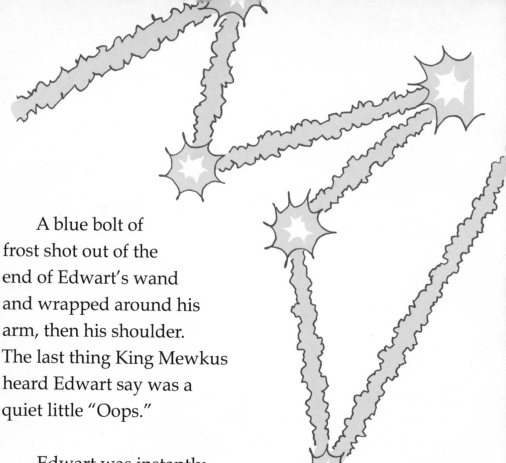

A blue bolt of
frost shot out of the
end of Edwart's wand
and wrapped around his
arm, then his shoulder.
The last thing King Mewkus
heard Edwart say was a
quiet little "Oops."

Edwart was instantly
covered in blue ice and
stood motionless like a statue.
He had frozen himself solid.

The wizard's frozen wand shot uncontrolled blasts of
ice bouncing around the room, causing the flustered king
to dodge each blast to avoid being frozen himself.

Pik and Flik unlocked the heavy wooden door of
the North Tower before the king could catch them. They
ducked through quickly and slammed it just as a stray
blast of ice covered the door in a thick sheet of solid ice.

Chapter 9

Standing in front of the giant cave opening, Rowland paused to remember his promise to the princess. The cool, stale breeze played with his hair as it drifted up from the murky blackness. "The dying breaths of a thousand long-departed souls," Rowland pondered. There was an unpleasant stench that floated up from the cave.

"UGH, what in the three kingdoms is that?" said Rowland.

Crustos sniffed at the air. "Smells like my dirty socks at the end of the month," he said with a grin.

Crustos hiked up his belt. "OK, boy, get ready. Did I mention the killer asthmatic bats that live in this cave?"

Rowland looked at Crustos. "Asthmatic bats? You mean bats with asthma? No, I think I would have remembered that."

"Yep," said Crustos. "Meanest beasties you've ever seen. All the time wheezing and gasping while they try to kill ya."

"How do you know all this stuff?" squeaked Rowland, exasperated. "Is there some monster guide book that I should know about?"

Crustos didn't answer. He continued peering into the dark cave opening . . . waiting.

Rowland put on his shoulder bag, checking inside to make sure his turtle was OK. "How're you doing in there, Angelina?" whispered Rowland into his bag.

Angelina was sleeping soundly at the bottom.

"She slept through all that spider craziness," said Rowland. "She's amazing."

Rowland picked up his Staff of Slumber and stepped deeper into the entrance of the cave. He felt a strange surge of confidence in his chest. He bent into a batter's pose and lifted his staff.

"OK, Crustos," said Rowland. "You make some noise, and when those bats come out, I'll whack them to sleep one by one. It'll be just like batting practice."

Rowland was loosening up his swing, smoothly rocking the staff back and forth, when a giant bat the size of a rhinoceros swooped out of the cave and grabbed him by the shirt. The monster lifted Rowland into the air as the terrified young knight thrashed his legs around helplessly.

"Ahhhhhhhhh! Help! It's BIG! It's a big bat!" screamed Rowland, as he frantically hit the bat with his Staff of Slumber over and over.

"Oh, I forgot to tell you, the bats are GIANT!" yelled Crustos from the ground. "Sorry. I totally should have mentioned that!"

Rowland dangled ten feet in the air from the bat's huge claws. "YES! All you said was asthma!"

Rowland continued hitting the bat. "Sleep! Why don't you sleep . . . SLEEP . . . SLEEP?"

Four more giant bats came out of the cave. They dove and swooped around Crustos. Poisonous drool dripped from their huge fangs. Their breath came with a horrible wheezing sound.

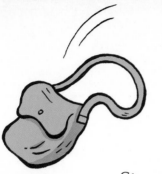

"Quick, throw me your bag, Rowland," screamed Crustos. "I have an idea."

Struggling against the monster bat, Rowland was able to remove the strap from around his shoulder. He tossed the bag to the old knight.

"Does your idea involve getting me down from here?" shouted Rowland. He continued hitting the bat with his staff, but the creature didn't even look sleepy.

Crustos caught Rowland's bag and jammed his arm inside, bringing sweet Angelina the turtle out in his hand.

The bat carrying Rowland swung around, and flew deeper into the cave. Its huge wings flapped and dipped around rocks and stalactites as they flew. Crustos ran along under them.

"Stop, bat!" cried Crustos.

"I don't think he's listening!" shouted Rowland.

Crustos ran at full speed right under the bat. He began shouting and holding Angelina up in the air to get the bat's attention.

"Look, bat! I have a tasty turtle! Don't you want this instead?" He held Angelina higher so the bat could see.

"No!" shouted Rowland, still hanging from the sharp claws of the bat. "I will not trade Angelina for myself! What are you doing? Stop!"

Rowland thrashed and struggled against the bat's tight grip. He could feel the bat's talons digging into his shoulders like knives.

Angelina looked wide awake now as Crustos ran along holding her up for the bat to eat. She looked up at the giant bat, confused. Rowland looked right at Angelina, and for a split second he saw anger flash in her eyes.

"Angelina, help!" cried Rowland.

Suddenly the dark passage was filled with blinding light and the most intense heat Rowland had ever felt. A thunderous explosion of fire filled the room. Rowland saw Crustos let go of Angelina and drop to the ground, rolling.

Fire was everywhere. Rowland felt himself fall, then roll hard against the dirt floor of the cave. He looked up to see Crustos huddled right next to him, covering his head.

Suddenly there was a terrible, wheezing yelp as the giant bats flew away. "Skaaaaaawwwwwk!"

Sweet Angelina was on the ground facing the retreating bats. Her mouth opened and another fiery blast of flame shot out, burning the wings of several more of the creatures. FOOOOOM!

"Skaaaaaawwwwwk! Skaaaaaawwwwwk!"

Then it was quiet. The bats were gone. Rowland crouched low in stunned silence. He tried to understand what had just happened.

"Angelina can breathe fire?" gasped Rowland.

"Ah-HAA!" yelled Crustos, happy to be alive. "I knew that little turtle was special as soon as I saw that mark on her shell!"

Rowland walked over and picked up his sweet Angelina. He stroked her shell lovingly. "Shhh, Angelina, it's OK. I'm safe now. Thank you for saving us." Her shell was very warm to the touch.

"That's an enchanted turtle, boy—extremely rare. Didn't you notice that symbol on her shell?"

"I was wondering what that was," beamed Rowland. "One day she was sunning herself in my field, just nibbling on my turnip plants. We've been friends ever since."

Angelina looked up at Rowland. Her eyes seemed to smile at him. The boy snuggled her close. Then Crustos tapped him on the shoulder.

"Uh, Rowland," said Crustos. "I don't think we're out of the soup just yet."

Rowland turned around to see what Crustos was looking at. In the archway of the dark cave behind them stood two enormous Nose Goblins. They looked very mad . . . and very hungry.

Chapter 10

Rowland and Crustos didn't panic when they saw the Nose Goblins. They were too stunned to react at all. The Nose Goblins were gigantic in every way. They were each at least twelve feet tall, and just as wide. They had large hands and feet, and their brutal faces had a pale green pallor. Snot ran from their enormous noses and dripped down around their mouths like gooey mustaches.

Fear began to sweep over Rowland, and he suppressed the urge to scream out. He imagined his feet nailed to the ground so he wouldn't run away. Brave knights do not run away. One of the goblins spoke out in a deep, stony voice.

"I want the fat one this time," said the goblin on the left.

"Excuse me," said the other goblin. "Last time I let you eat the horse, too, remember? I say we split fat one in half and flip coin for the little one. That fair."

"WE ARE THE KNIGHTS OF BOO'GAR!" screamed Rowland, unexpectedly. "AND WE DEMAND THAT YOU YIELD TO US!"

Crustos looked at Rowland like he was crazy. "Uh . . . what my little friend means is," Crustos spoke politely, "we'd like very much to speak with you for a moment, and then we'll be on our way."

Crustos leaned close to Rowland. "Cool it, kid. These guys are giants. Show a little respect."

Rowland leaned in and whispered, "Yes, I figured that these guys would be giant, and they are. Those bats were a total surprise."

"Look," growled Crustos out of the side of his mouth, "I already apologized about the bats and the spiders. Can we just drop it?"

"Stop talking, small people!" said left goblin. "We already know why you are here. You come to pick fruit of the Handsome Tree."

"No," said Rowland. "We just want our goat back. So if you . . ."

Crustos interrupted. "Wait. You have a Handsome Tree?"

The right goblin then spoke. "What goat you talking about? You are confusing me and Juan."

"Who's Juan?" asked Rowland.

"I am Juan," said Juan. "And this is my brother, Tony. We have names and feelings just like you. We not just scary plot device."

"I'm so sorry, Juan," Rowland apologized. "I didn't mean to imply anything. This all seems to be a big misunderstanding."

"So, you don't know anything about a goat?" asked Crustos.

The goblins looked at each other and shrugged.

Crustos thought for a moment, then he took the Orb of Seeing out of his bag and studied it. The image in the orb was foggy and vague, and there was no goat in the picture.

"That's funny," said Crustos. "This enchanted orb plainly showed us the goat in this cave. Now it's showing us nothing."

Rowland stroked his freckled chin.

"It doesn't make sense," said Rowland. "We both saw Babycakes in the orb. He has to be here."

Rowland stood in the gloom of the cave, puzzling over the situation. Angelina waited. Juan scratched his belly.

"Sir Crustos," said Rowland, "where did you say you got that orb?"

"I told you. A couple of traveling monks," said Crustos. "It was a really great deal. At least I thought it was." He shook the orb.

"Monks?" gasped Rowland. "Were they wearing green robes by any chance?"

"I think so, yes. I . . ."

"Was one of them kind of a tall, hipster-looking dude?" Rowland pressed excitedly.

"Excuse us," said Tony the goblin, "we don't mean to interrupt your nice conversation, but we hungry. So it's time to eat you guys."

Just then, the wall next to the goblins trembled and cracked. There was a terrible rumbling sound. Rocks and dust started falling from the ceiling and the ground shook like an earthquake. The two knights and the two goblins braced themselves against the floor to keep from toppling over.

CRASSHHHHH! went the wall, as a huge hole opened up, sending boulders tumbling into the cave with a horrific, thunderous BOOM!

"HI, BOYS!" said a female voice from high atop a huge mechanical monster. "Anyone wanna get rescued?"

Chapter 11

The princess had arrived in Boo'Gar's steam-powered harvesting robot. It had two mechanical legs and big claws at the end of long extendable brass arms. She sat in a cockpit protected by an ornate iron cage decorated with colorful translucent jewels.

Rowland's face brightened. "Well, hi there, Princess! How did you find us?"

The princess pulled some levers and a blast of hot vapor shot out of the back of the robot. Its engines whirred and rumbled to a stop.

"I borrowed some doodad from the wizard that lets me track magical objects on my KPS," said the princess.

She held up a small brass box with blinking blue lights and a short antenna. "Kingdom positioning system. See? I just tracked your Staff of Slumber to this cave."

The princess looked down at the Nose Goblins. "How come we're not fighting these monsters? Why is everyone just standing around? Where is my goat?"

"It seems that there's been a mix-up," said Rowland. "They don't have Babycakes. Pik and Flik, those two green monks from your castle, gave us a fake Orb of Seeing." He pointed to Sir Crustos. "It sent us both out here on this phony goat chase."

The princess noticed old Crustos standing there. "Pleased to meet you, good Sir Knight. My father thanks you for your service."

Crustos blushed a deep red and bent into a crooked bow. "Honored to be of service, My Lady."

FFT

Phlema climbed down from her robot and stood next to Rowland. She felt her anger rising. "So it was those two annoying monks the whole time! They kidnapped my darling?"

Rowland nodded.

"THOSE CREEPS!" exploded Princess Phlema. "How are we going to find Babycakes now?"

Juan the goblin spoke up. "I can't believe I say this, but I think we can help you. Tony and I have magical object much better than Orb of Seeing. We have Globe of Watching," he said proudly. "Much more accurate. Very high-end."

"Yes," said Tony, the other goblin. "We'll find your goat, and then you can go wreck someone else's living room."

"THAT'S PERFECT! What are we waiting for?" shouted Phlema.

"OK, but please take loud princess with you when you go," said Tony.

Juan and Tony led the group to the back of their cave and up onto a stone altar. The altar was lit with torches on all sides, and sweet-smelling incense burned in a small pot. In the middle of the altar was a stone column holding up a large golden-colored glass ball.

Rowland, Crustos, and Phlema gathered together around the Globe of Watching, set deep into the ancient stone stand. Juan and Tony hunched over the globe and began to move their hands over its surface.

A sharp moving image appeared immediately in the glass globe.

"Wow, he's right," said Rowland. "That's a much better picture!"

"That's high-definition, boy," said Crustos. "I'd love to have one of these babies back at my place."

"Be quiet, you bozos!" yelled Phlema. "I mean . . . good sir knights. I'm trying to see."

They all watched the scene of King Mewkus chasing Pik and Flik through the castle into the tower. Flik was clearly carrying a goat-shaped bundle.

NYAAA!

"That's him!" said Princess Phlema. "He has Babycakes. He was in the castle the entire time!"

"We have to get back to Boo'Gar and help your dad!" cried Rowland. "Uh, I mean the king."

The two Nose Goblins, Juan and Tony, waved their hands to shut off the Globe of Watching, then stepped off the altar.

Rowland felt angry and helpless. It would take days to get back to Boo'Gar, and by then the criminal monks would be long gone. He had completely traveled in the wrong direction, and now the princess might lose her goat. Being a knight was harder than he thought.

While Phlema and the two knights wondered what to do, Juan and Tony stood whispering in the corner. Then they turned back to the group, and Juan cleared his throat loudly. "Uh . . . ahem," he said.

"Tony and I have decided—we go back with you to help you defeat these mean people. We know a good short-cut that will get you back to castle in about fifteen minutes," he said proudly.

Tony spoke up next. "Yes, we can float down the roaring rapids of the Loogey River all the way to Boo'Gar. But Juan and I can't swim, so that might be big problem."

"That's not a problem!" yelled Princess Phlema. "My harvester has inflatable pontoons. I added them during one really rainy season we had," she said excitedly. "We can float down the river!"

Rowland turned to Juan and Tony. "Thank you, guys. But why are you willing to help us after we bashed your cave to smithereens?"

"We have stayed in this cave for many years," said Juan earnestly. "People used to throw rocks and spears at us because we are ugly. If we let people know we are nice . . ."

"Yes," said Tony. "Townsfolk will learn that we are friends to the people of Boo'Gar. We can leave cave again, maybe go out for a nice pizza dinner."

The Loogey River was just a short walk away along the cliffs. A bright sun hung high in the clear sapphire-blue sky. Juan and Tony didn't look any less monstrous in full sunlight, but Sir Crustos kept everyone busy making preparations for the journey home.

The group quickly gathered some supplies. When Tulip the ostrich spotted Rowland coming out of the cave, she ran over to him and gave him a sticky kiss on the cheek. There were half-eaten cantaloupe rinds everywhere. She was clearly feeling much better.

"Hi there, Tulip!" said Rowland, hugging her around the neck. "Did you miss me?"

After snuggling with Rowland, Tulip looked up and noticed the giant Nose Goblins standing there. She let out a frightened "Skweeeeep!"

The goblins led them down to an opening in the rock. A raging torrent of foamy water blasted out from under the white marble. The cold, clear water then emptied into a deep river, stretching to the horizon. The great Loogey River.

"OK, let me inflate the pontoons," shouted the princess. "Back up, everyone!"

She pulled a few levers and then pushed the red button that said INFLATE.

They saw blasts of steam and heard low hissing sounds as large rubber balloons inflated from beneath the robot.

Rowland checked his bag to make sure he still had Angelina and his Staff of Slumber. Angelina looked up at him and batted her eyes playfully.

"Don't worry, Angelina," said Rowland with a smile. "I'm not letting you out of my sight again."

As everyone was climbing in the raft, Crustos had a last-minute idea. "Juan and Tony, can you carry some of these ripe cantaloupes back with us? We need to show the king how well his crops are doing," said Crustos. "Just use your shirt like a basket."

Juan and Tony gathered a pile of cantaloupes into their shirts and climbed awkwardly into the robot harvester. It bobbed and dipped very low in the water under the enormous weight, but stayed afloat.

"OK, is everyone ready?" shouted Phlema. "Here we go!"

She pushed off from the bank of the river, and immediately the group was swept away in the icy current. They bounced along violently, crashing through the rapids. Waves pounded the sides of their makeshift little boat.

"Wooooooo!" shouted Phlema above the roar of the churning water. "Babycakes, here we come!"

Rowland hung on for dear life, squeezing his eyes tight when he began to feel seasick. He wondered if they should have ignored Juan and Tony's shortcut advice. "This would be a very silly way for a knight to come to his end," Rowland thought to himself.

After a mile or so, the river calmed down and Rowland began to relax. He opened his eyes and watched the beautiful mountains and green fields of Boo'Gar pass by. Rowland decided that he had been wrong to think about staying on his farm forever. Now that he had traveled across miles of Boo'Gar countryside, he was truly, deeply proud of the kingdom he called home.

Chapter 12

The wizard Edwart was still shaking off the effects of the freeze spell when he staggered up to King Mewkus. The king sat leaning against the frozen tower door, feeling sorry for himself.

"Your Highness," gasped the wizard, "what are you doing? Where are those two dishonest monks, Pik and Flik?"

"I couldn't catch them," The king sighed. "They got into the tower and now they're in there with the book and the goat."

King Mewkus looked up at his friend Edwart, still covered in melting ice flakes. "Nice job on the freeze spell, by the way," grumbled the king playfully.

"It's my new wand," explained Edwart. "I told the wandmaker that I wanted the handle to be much wider, but the top of the wand looks just like the handle, and I didn't have my glasses . . ."

"Never mind that now," grunted the king. He dragged himself up off the floor and brushed off his robes. "Let's get Babycakes back, shall we?"

King Mewkus had had enough. He was tired of being the lame king of a pitiful kingdom. He was tired of nothing ever going right. This time, he was going to win. He wasn't going to take no for an answer.

The king pulled his friend close. "Edwart, gather whatever men you can find. Then go find something to chop through this ice."

Just as Edwart turned to leave, there was a horrible scream from just outside the castle.

"Eeeeeeeek!"

Edwart and King Mewkus ran to investigate. A small crowd had gathered in the courtyard at the foot of the tower.

"What's going on here?" asked the king.

"Your Majesty," said a frightened handmaiden. "Up in the tower . . . they've got Babycakes!"

The king looked up and gasped. Flik the monk was holding Babycakes out the window of the tall tower. "Nyaaaaa!" said the poor, frightened little goat.

"We have Babycakes," shouted Flik. "And we have the *Book of Loogey*. Allow us safe passage to Sneezix and we won't throw Babycakes from this tower."

"Sneezix!" growled King Mewkus. He felt his temper rise once again. "So, it was King Sinius who put you up to this, you scoundrels! Tell me, what did Sinius offer you to betray your kingdom and steal our treasured book?"

"A ticket out of this fleabag kingdom, for starters," Flik spat with contempt.

King Mewkus was quickly losing his patience. "Return Babycakes peacefully and you won't be hurt."

Flik disappeared from the window for a moment. The crowd looked up, waiting. He reemerged, holding a flaming torch next to the *Book of Loogey*. The crowd lost their collective giblets.

"NOOOOOO!" they screamed.

The king pointed his finger up at Flik. "Don't you dare harm that book!" The situation had escalated very quickly.

Flik menacingly waved the torch around. Its flames grew larger and began to creep down the handle of the torch. The crowd held their hands over their mouths and watched helplessly.

Flik screamed, "I will do it! I'll set the book on fire. You better get us out of here and let us go!"

The king noticed that the smoke from the torch was gathering under the dry, thatched roof of the tower.

"Be careful!" screamed the king. "The tower roof will catch—"

FOOOM! The roof burst into flames and, suddenly, the tower was burning.

Flik looked up at the flames, and the color drained from his face. When Pik appeared next to him in the window, the two monks had a heated conversation.

Pik looked down at the king. "AHHHHHH! UMM, we give up! We're coming down!"

"Wait! You can't," shouted Edwart. "My spell froze the door shut behind you. It'll take hours to chop through that ice!"

"You can't be serious," screamed Pik. "We'll be burned alive!"

The flames surged across the roof of the tower. Thick smoke was now billowing out of the tower windows, and everyone could hear the two monks coughing and hacking.

"H . . . cough . . . Heelllp! Cough . . . cough."

"Hang on a minute! I'm thinking!" yelled the king. Suddenly, there was another sharp shriek from the crowd.

"Eeeeeeek!"

The handmaiden was now pointing to the outer walls of the castle. Edwart, the king, and the rest of the villagers turned to see what she was looking at.

A giant pair of horrible twelve-foot Nose Goblins came hopping over the wall carrying about twelve thousand cantaloupes. Princess Phlema came over next driving a giant robot with inflatable pontoons, followed by the Knights of Boo'Gar riding an ostrich and carrying a fire-breathing turtle.

"Well . . . this day just keeps getting more and more interesting," the king said calmly.

Phlema and her mechanical harvester came to a halt right in front of the king. "Where's Babycakes?!" screamed Phlema. "Why is the tower on fire? What's going on?"

"Up there," shouted the wizard. "The door is frozen shut and he'll be burned up if we don't do something."

Rowland and Crustos rode up on Tulip and then hopped off in opposite directions, landing perfectly. "We've got to get that fire out," shouted Rowland. "Princess, can you use your robot's arms to raise me up above the tower?"

"Yes," she said. "The arms extend like a ladder!"

Rowland climbed into one of the robot's metal hands. He took his Staff of Slumber out of his bag and held on tightly.

"OK, Princess," said Rowland. "Let's do this!"

The princess pulled some levers and the robot arm slowly rose into the air. Rowland went higher and higher. He clung to one of the robot fingers as he soared into the smoky afternoon sky, finally stopping with a jolt just above the burning tower roof. The heat was intense.

Rowland got into his batter's stance and called down to Juan and Tony. "OK, boys! Batter up! Throw those melons at me!"

Juan was first to pick up a cantaloupe. He drew back his arm and threw as hard as he could.

WHOOOSH!

The cantaloupe did a long, gentle arc directly at Rowland, who was waiting with a look of intense concentration. At just the right moment, he swung.

BLLAAAAPH! went the cantaloupe, as Rowland splattered it into a million juicy bits that rained down on the fire. The bits of melon sizzled as they landed on the burning roof.

"More!" screamed Rowland. "Keep them coming!"

The king could barely see Rowland through the blanket of black smoke that engulfed the tower, but he could hear Babycakes bleating and crying in fear. He knew that he couldn't wait for the fire to go out. The king had to do something to save Babycakes.

Juan and Tony threw as fast as they could, and Rowland smacked each cantaloupe with exact precision, sending showers of juice down over the tower.

BLLAAAAPH! BLLAAAAPH! BLLAAAAPH!

The king ran to the foot of the tower, directly under the window, and shouted up to the kidnappers. "There's no time. Throw me the goat!"

Pik came to the window with Babycakes in his arms. He let go and the goat was suddenly falling like a rock . . . or like a goat.

"Babycakes!" screamed Princess Phlema.

The sweet goat dropped through the air as if in slow motion. His little legs wiggled and kicked as he fell, and the crowd of villagers held their breath.

Brave King Mewkus, his arms outstretched, caught the little animal perfectly.

"Gotcha," said the king. The crowd erupted in a huge cheer.

"Hooraaay!"

Rowland whacked a few more cantaloupes, and the fire was slowly overwhelmed by sweet cantaloupe juice. Finally, it fizzled out completely.

The roof of the tower was a smoking ruin. White smoke curled into the evening sky above the two monks. Flik and Pik stood, covered in soot, looking down at the crowd below.

Pik cradled the *Book of Loogey* in his arms. "Can we come down now? Cough . . . cough."

Chapter 13

Rowland was lowered down to the ground to join King Mewkus and the small group that had gathered outside the tower door. The fire had not completely melted the ice, and the door remained frozen shut.

"Father," said Princess Phlema. "I'd like to introduce you to one of your brave Boo'Gar knights. This is Sir Crustos. He helped us get back in time." The king bowed to Crustos.

"Twas my honor, Your Majesty," said Crustos. "I'll have that door open in five minutes with my trusty axe."

Crustos removed his axe from his pack and held it nervously. It had been a few years since he had wielded the weapon, and it was covered in rust and grime.

"Here goes nothing," chirped the knight cheerfully.

He drew the axe back and swung a mighty blow against the frozen ice-covered door.

THUNK! went the axe as it stuck deep into the ice. Crustos yanked the axe free and, with great effort, took another mighty swing.

CRASH! The ice shattered into a million pieces and fell to the floor.

The crowd cheered, "Hooraaay!"

Crustos blushed with embarrassment. "All in a day's work. No big deal." He looked down at his blade and noticed a change.

The impact of the ice had knocked the rust and dirt off the old blade. It looked as new as the day it was forged. The steel gleamed in the sunlight, and the blade looked razor sharp again. Crustos felt a rush of pride fill his heart.

With the door open, Pik and Flik staggered out of the tower. Crustos grabbed them roughly by the shirt collar and led them both over to the king.

The king gently took the treasure from them and flicked off a few specks of soot. It appeared to be undamaged. It was now up to him and the princess to determine an appropriate punishment for the two scheming monks.

Phlema spoke plainly. "Don't go easy on them, Father. After all, they are traitors."

"King Mewkus, sir," said Rowland. "You have a gigantic cantaloupe field out beyond the Valley of Spiders. I think these felonious monks should work in your fields as penance for their evil deeds."

The king liked this idea very much. He turned to the two monks, who looked very sorry for the big mess they had caused.

"Pik and Flik, you kidnapped my daughter's goat and lied to us," the king said sternly. "You also conspired with King Sinius to steal the *Book of Loogey*. So I sentence both of you to three years of labor, working in the newly discovered cantaloupe fields beyond the Valley of Spiders."

Crustos nudged the two prisoners. "Yes, and good luck getting there," he chuckled. "You might want to bring along some bug spray, hee-hee."

"Take them away, Sir Crustos," said the king.

The princess and the king watched as the two monks were led into the castle for safekeeping.

The wizard Edwart walked up to young Sir Rowland. "So, Sir Rowland, how did that Staff of Slumber work out for you?"

Rowland smiled. "It's just a stick, isn't it?"

"On the contrary, my dear fellow. It's quite magical. How else could Phlema track you down?"

"So . . . it *is* enchanted?" asked Rowland.

"Well, it transformed you into a knight, didn't it?" The old wizard smiled broadly. "Sometimes the best magic is a little dose of confidence, hmm?"

Rowland took Angelina the turtle out of his bag to show the wizard. "It doesn't hurt to have friends, either."

Angelina batted her eyes and spat out a little bubble of fire to delight the crowd.

"Extraordinary!" said the king. He put his arm around Rowland. "I couldn't ask for two better knights."

The two Nose Goblins, Juan and Tony, made themselves useful by picking up pieces of cantaloupe and stacking the remaining melons into a neat pile.

A tall figure stepped out of the crowd of villagers. He wore the expensive robes of a merchant and spoke in a clear, friendly voice.

"Brave King Mewkus. My name is Lord Lewis Loganberry," he said with a smile. "I am a fruit dealer from an island not far from here. I would like to buy this remaining pile of cantaloupes for ten thousand pieces of gold."

"You've got a deal!" said the king. The two men shook hands.

Lord Loganberry continued. "I would very much like to be your exclusive cantaloupe salesman throughout the kingdoms. If your cantaloupe fields are as big as they say, I think you will soon become a very, very wealthy kingdom."

The crowd cheered. "Hooray for brave King Mewkus!"

Princess Phlema gave her dad a high-five. Rowland did a fist bump with Edwart. The setting sun was turning the sky to a cantaloupe shade of red-orange, and everyone felt a little more hopeful and a little more excited about the future of Boo'Gar.

THE END

(for now)

Medieval Devices

There may not have been steam-powered cantaloupe harvesters in the real Middle Ages, but there were plenty of cool devices used every day around the castle.

Medieval Devices

Treadwheel Crane

A human-powered wooden crane designed to lift heavy objects. Operated by a person walking in a big hamster wheel, turning a spindle attached to a pulley system. The rotation of the wheel caused the spindle to turn, lifting or lowering the heavy object.

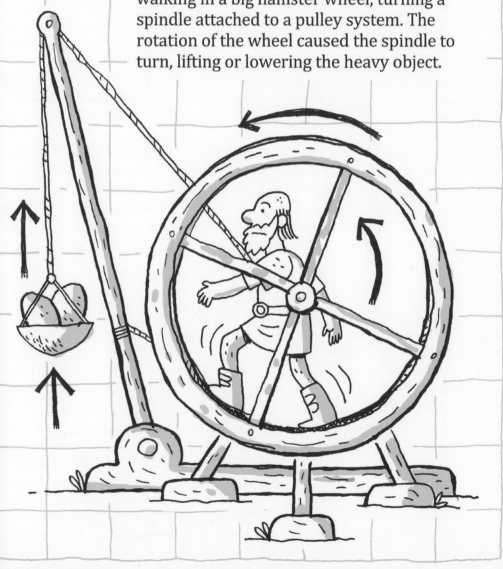

Medieval Devices

Builder's Level

Even ancient castles had to be built on a straight line. When laying bricks or carving huge stones, the castle builders could use this device to determine if a wall was level. A small weight attached to a string hung straight down. If it didn't tilt to one side or the other, the wall was level.

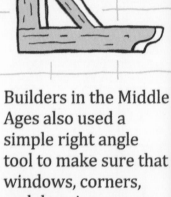

Builders in the Middle Ages also used a simple right angle tool to make sure that windows, corners, and door jams were straight.

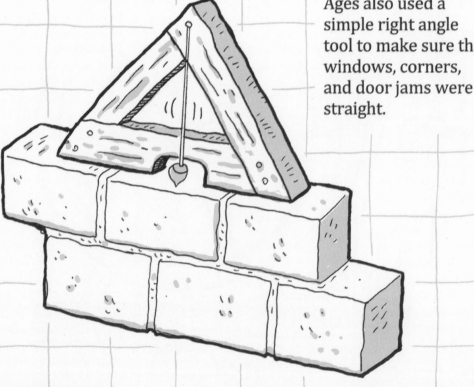

Medieval Devices

Trebuchet

Pronounced Tre-Bew-Shay, this Middle Age war machine used a heavy counter-weight for power. When the weight was dropped, it would swing down with great force, causing the other end of the arm to throw huge objects as far as 300 meters.

After throwing a boulder or flaming ball of tar (or a dead cow), the arm could be cranked back into position and fired again.

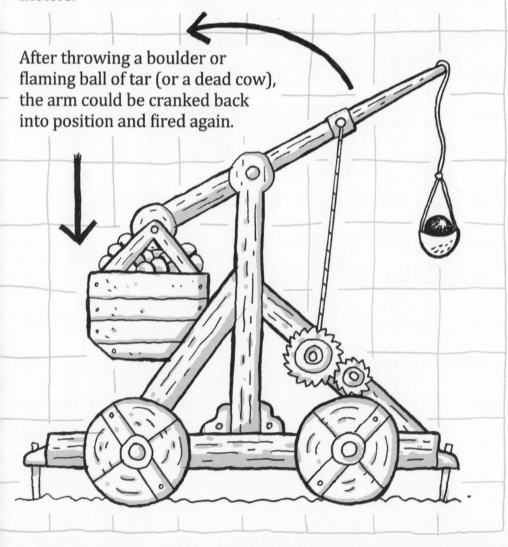

Medieval Devices

Ballista

In ancient times the ballista was basically a cannon that shot a very heavy pointed projectile. It was a very clever device that used two levers twisted with rope until they were wound extremely tight like a spring. Then they were cranked back, and an arrow or rock was placed in the firing channel. When the lever arms were released, the weapon fired with great force.